THE FAIRY TALES OF AMBROSE

Amphibians
AND
Admiration

A FROG PRINCE RETELLING

AMANDA THOMPSON

DEDICATION

To the wonderful ladies of Once Upon a Pen,

Thank you for your encouragement and support. Hazel's story would have remained hidden in my mind forever if not for you; she would have been just a small piece of another girl's tale.

CONTENTS

CHAPTER ONE
AN UNFULFILLED WISH

"Are you listening?"

I barely notice my sister's question as I had just been staring out the window, thinking how lovely it would be to be in the gardens at this moment. I would choose the stone garden for a day like today, imagining a new story for each of the statues placed in it.

Gardenia whispered in such a low voice that nobody else in the meeting heard. Her tone warns me. I have been lost in my thoughts for far too long. However, I struggle with paying attention and that leads to me feeling guilty because the day is so beautiful and warm. We haven't yet reached the hotter days when everyone prefers to be near a shady tree or cool lake.

Gardenia is giving me a look that speaks volumes about how unhappy she is with me. I suppress a sigh. I detest these council meetings. It becomes increasingly difficult for me to pay attention when boredom sets in. Is it my fault when the sky looks so inviting? I aspire to be free from all this mind-numbing paperwork and endless list of meetings.

"Is it necessary for me to listen to them talk for hours when we both know you understand all of this better than I do?" I reply to my sister in a hushed tone.

"You. Are. The. Heir!" From her exasperated whispers, I can tell she is upset with me. I do not blame her. Her demeanor is calmer and more reserved when there are people who are not family present.

What I said is true, though. Nia understands the trade agreements, laws, and traditions of not only Verdant, but all the kingdoms of the continent of Ambrose. I am in awe of her ability to remember it all and keep it straight. She is the natural choice for the next queen of Verdant.

I have studied the history of the kingdom and there has been one time an heir gave up the throne. So, that sets a precedent, but I do not believe Father will go for this option. He does not see things the way I do. And I am too afraid to say anything. I do not want to disappoint him any more than I already have. Sadly, that is a truth my father is too blind to see—or he is refusing to acknowledge.

Gardenia has the knowledge and the will, and she loves learning about and doing the things the heir to the throne is supposed to do, while I would rather travel to the different kingdoms on our continent and experience what each culture offers. I want to be free; and in the deepest, darkest parts of my heart, I want my sister to be the queen after our father.

The lord speaking at this council meeting is discussing the finances of our beautiful kingdom. He is not looking in my direction, so what caused Gardenia to notice my lack of attention? I discreetly turn my head about the council meeting room and see my father giving me an angry look. *Ahh, that's it.* Why can't Father understand I love our kingdom and people, but I want something different? Maybe an adventure. He has plenty of daughters to select a different heir from.

The council meeting room is next to Father's office. After this meeting, Father will summon me there, as he does at the end of each meeting, so Gardenia and I can report our thoughts to him. Gardenia usually has more to say because she is the one that pays attention.

Glancing between Father and Gardenia, I take in the scene. I could envy my sister, but I do not. I am happy that one of us can do the things that need to be done. The council meeting does not last much longer and, without a word to the council members, Nia and I leave our desks in the back of the room and make our way to Father's office. We each take a seat across from his desk.

"Was anything crucial spoken of in today's meeting?" I murmur to my sister. She gives me a pitiful look and makes herself comfortable in her chair she is sitting in before answering me.

"Yes, the heir of Cortes is missing and presumed to be dead," she says sadly. I perk up at this interesting information. Not because I wish anything ill to happen to him, but this is so much more exciting than the trade profits we presently receive. "And it caused a stir in the council meeting with the fear that dark magic is making a rise again."

"What do you mean by 'presumed dead'?" I ask. I should not be eager, but my chances for adventure are only by learning about someone else's. "And is there a likely chance that dark magic is getting stronger?"

"He was part of a search effort of some sort, and then he, along with his entire squadron, went missing. There is no trace of them, and everyone presumes they are dead. It is quite sad and truly terrifying. There was talk of asking a mage with light magic to come address the council. However, a few of the members did not like the idea because no other kingdom seems to have issues with dark magic. And sadly, yes, I know that none of the kingdoms have faced anything truly serious in over three hundred.years

Not since the Frozen Queen was destroyed in Norland back then."

"Yes, terrifying," I tell her, barely hearing the rest of what she says, imagining what sort of adventure the prince could be on. I genuinely hope he is on an adventure and nothing worse than that has happened to him. But if he is on an adventure, rogue agents could be holding him, wanting to ransom him. Or he could be a victim of a dastardly, villainous mage's curse.

My mind continues to race with all the things he could face until my father slams a heavy book on his desk. From the look on his face, he has been trying to get my attention. My tendency to get easily distracted is a failing. But thinking of the heir of Cortes's potential adventures is exciting.

"Sorry," I mumble to him. I cannot help but feel guilty as I meet Father's angry gaze.

"Honestly, Hazel. I am not sure what to do with you," Father says with more than a little exasperation. I understand, I do; it must be frustrating to have your heir be so disinterested in everything. Maybe he will finally bring up naming Nia as heir? I would sign over my birthright to her in a heartbeat.

My sister, being the perfect heir, should give me the freedom to be myself. To leave and go on adventures. To tell the man I like, and perhaps love, that I want a future with him. But I lack the bravery to articulate these things, to say how I honestly feel. Maybe one day I will.

"Father," Gardenia starts, but she stops speaking at the angry look on his face. She is the younger sister. Instead of protecting her, it is the younger sister who is always defending and looking out for the older one.

"I am sorry for not paying attention to the meeting, Father," I say to him. I open my mouth to continue my apology, but he raises a hand to stop me.

"This is not working, Hazel. You are using your sister. She has her own duties she is supposed to be attending. She has not even finished all her schooling yet. But Gardenia is the one who pays attention to what is said in each meeting. And more importantly, what is not being said. What do we need to do to get you to focus? To do what you need to do?" Father's deep voice is full of exasperation and anger.

"I—" I badly want to tell him the truth, but will that only make things worse? "I don't know," I finally answer him. *Why won't you speak up for yourself, Hazel? Speak your mind!* I berate myself and prepare the words to say all day, but I cannot vocalize them. I do not aspire to be the heir. It is a mistake, yet I struggle to utter the words.

I do not have the passion, drive, or love for duties like Gardenia.

"You don't know?" Father asks darkly. "Perhaps I should hire more tutors for you? Maybe one of them will make you interested in your responsibilities?"

"No, dearest, that will not work," Sabrina, Father's wife, says from the doorway of the office. Closing the door behind her, she walks across the room to where the three of us are seated. I like Sabrina. She brings out the gentle side of Father. If true love is real, then Sabrina and Father have that. And I am glad because even though I miss my mother, I do not want Father to be alone and miserable. "Maybe not having Nia to fall back on would be a better incentive," Sabrina continues.

"Yes," Father says, agreeing with my stepmother. *Wait. Why do I like her again?* Nia looks hurt at the suggestion, but I know she will not say a word. After all, she is the perfect princess.

Oh, that is an unkind thought, and my sister does not deserve it. She volunteered to go to the council meetings on her own, not because she wanted to show me up, but because she wanted to help me. She enjoys the meetings, though I know part of her reasoning was because of how I struggled. Nia asks questions where I usually stare out the window.

I love Sabrina. I truly do. She is father's third wife. My mother, his first wife, died giving birth to the twins, Lily and Lavender. Father's second wife died from an illness. But his childhood friend and was there each time my father had his heart broken. I believe she has loved my father since childhood and maybe even swore off relationships with other men because of it. As the oldest, I have memories of my mother and first stepmother, and their deaths. Sabrina never tried to replace them but to be there for father and us girls.

"And I think we will need to choose prospective suitors soon," Father adds. My heart sinks to my toes, because I doubt my father will ever consider Roderick, a junior ambassador. The boy, now a man, who stole my heart years ago. We started out as friends. Then, just when I thought we could be more, he left for his duties. He would be gone for weeks or months at a time because of his training and travels. To this day, he is the only man who has made my heart skip a beat, and it's his face I dream of whenever he is away from court for his duties as junior ambassador. I know that as a royal from Verdant, my children will most likely inherit the green eyes of the royal family. But is it crazy that I want to see little cherub-faced toddlers with my blonde curls and his wonderful coffee brown eyes?

"How did today's meeting go?" Nia asks me after the council meeting. We are sitting in the shared sitting room designated for all of us princesses. She hasn't been allowed in a council meeting for months. I continue to struggle as badly as I always have, but today was not as big of a problem. I enjoyed the meeting. Roderick and the other ambassadors spoke for most of the meeting. I make myself comfortable in my favorite chair by the fireplace before answering her.

"Apparently, the heir of Cortes has been found, and he is now happily engaged to the new Duchess of Carabas," I answer her, hoping she might ask more questions so I can tell her all the things that were discussed in today's meeting.

"Truly?" Nia asks curiously. She typically conceals her emotions well, but with just the two of us in the sitting room tonight, she can show her curiosity about my news.

"Yes, according to the reports given today, Cortes had a dark mage problem. A sorcerer with successful power was slowly turning all the people in the kingdom into dark, nasty versions of themselves. He also turned a squadron of guards to stone and the heir into a cat. A miller's daughter defeated him." I spoke so fast because of my excitement. I am not sure that Nia understood what I was saying until she asks me about the miller's daughter.

"A miller's daughter? Then why is the prince marrying a duchess? Isn't that how these things usually work?"

Buzzing with excitement, I can finally report on a council meeting, and I have my sister's full attention! I realize I am bouncing on my seat and stop. Immediately. Nia smiles at me from her favorite chair just across from me beside the fireplace. Her chair, a lovely wingback, has undergone multiple refurbishments because of many years of use. It used to be our mother's chair.

"The new duchess *is* the miller's daughter!" I squeal my reply. "But can you imagine the adventure that must have happened for her to go from miller's daughter to duchess and future queen?"

"It must have been quite exciting," Nia says softly. "She must be very brave."

"Yes." I pause before revealing this next truth to my sister. "I am actually jealous of her." I look out the window behind Gardenia. The window is massive, and all I can see are the moon and stars. "Do you remember when we would wish upon stars?" I whisper to her, changing the subject again. I can hear her move from her chair and walk the short distance to mine. She kneels in front of me and delicately takes my hand.

"I understand envying someone having what you want," she whispers. Our sisters are in their rooms and our lady's maids are waiting for us in our suites, but Nia, being the kind of person she is, says this so that no one else can overhear us. "As for making wishes. Well, I have never stopped," she says nicely and gets up. She says goodnight and leaves the room.

She is right. Perhaps I should wish on a star. What is the worst thing that could happen? That it does not come true? I tiptoe to the balcony outside of our sitting room. It has a fantastic view of the night sky. I step up to the balcony's banister and look out at the garden below. Different gardens surround our castle, though we still have expansive grounds for many events and parties and such. We are incredibly lucky to live here. And I am going to try my luck with a wish. I admire the alluringly dark sky. A strong breeze loosens my updo, but I welcome it as the heat of the summer day lingers. Verdant, like many of our neighbors, has long summers and short winters, giving us a good growing season. The unfortunate side effect is the long, hot days.

I choose a star that has the greatest twinkle and close my eyes to make my wish.

"Oh, star shining bright, I hope you grant this wish tonight." I take a deep breath and continue. "That I may relinquish the throne for an adventure with my true love."

I open my eyes, which are now wet, and can see the star twinkling above in the blue. I hope this does not become another unfulfilled wish.

Chapter Two

An Unwelcome Companion

Winter has arrived, and Father has finally consented to Gardenia's return to the council meetings. Three full seasons have passed. Seasons of me giving dismal reports on the meetings. I am glad she may attend once more. But I believe the only reason Father has allowed her to return is because he wants me to focus on selecting a ... *suitor.*

Sabrina and Father found three young Verdant men they believe will match me and help me be the best queen possible. Candidate Number One is Conrad Ryan, a count's son. His family is very wealthy; however, Conrad is a toad, thanks to his personality and attitude. He would be attractive if not for the nastier side of his temperament. I am not sure how many of the nobility have noticed that about him. However, it does not stop the young ladies of the court from vying for his attention.

The second candidate is Ronald. He is also wealthy with land, but no title. If I were to marry him, he would bring more financial stability to Verdant, but nothing else. Also, Ronald reminds me of a cat because he is constantly jumping at his own shadow. The man is a coward. He is a gentle soul, but I am not sure if he would be a strong consort.

Third is Anthony. Not wealthy but has a title—he is a duke. I believe him to be too young for me as he is sixteen, and I am twenty-one. All the interactions I have had with Anthony have been awkward. He is the kindest of all three suitors, but he is so bashful and blushes red every time I speak to him. He reminds me of a turtle that wants to remain in its shell.

The awful part of all of this is that I think Roderick knows of my feelings and might return them. My parents will not consider him because he is not titled or from a wealthy family. However, he is one of my oldest friends. We met as children and became fast companions. He was the first person other than Gardenia who I shared my dreams of traveling with. We used to talk about the things we would see and where we would go. He was the one I always hoped to have adventures with. And I think he might want the same with me, even still. Instead, this evening my companion will be Conrad.

Conrad is joining my parents and me in our private box at the theater. I had pleaded with my parents to allow Gardenia to join us, but they would not hear a word about it.

As I step off the stairs onto the ground floor near the main entrance, a soothing voice pulls me from my dreary thoughts. "Evening, Princess."

I turn towards the speaker, and my heart skips a beat when my eyes meet his. Roderick is in the entryway; he looks wonderful in his suit. Forget butterflies. Hummingbirds are trying to take flight in my stomach. When he smiles at me, I feel like the only person in the room.

"Evening, Junior Ambassador," I say when I step off the last stair and give him a curtsy. He bows to me, and I can look up at him, as I am the shortest of the grown daughters. Before either of us can say anything else, though, Conrad interrupts us.

"There you are, Princess," Conrad says snidely. He does not bow to me or show any recognition of Roderick.

"Lord Ryan," I address him coolly. I glance back at Roderick, and he is frowning in Conrad's direction. Roderick changes his expression when he notices my attention on him.

"Are you ready to go?" Conrad asks me. "My carriage awaits."

"Sorry?" I ask him politely because I know I will ride to and from the theater with my parents, and he will not be in the carriage.

"Are. You. Ready?" Conrad repeats his question as if I am too dimwitted to have understood him the first time.

"I will ride with my family, as you know, Lord Ryan. And we will see you at the theater." The arrogant jerk does not deserve my kind tone, but I want him to know that I will not be alone with him.

"Yes, I was about to escort the princess to her parents when you appeared," Roderick says darkly. *Am I crazy? Because I loved that!*

"No need, Abbott. I can escort the princess," Conrad says dismissively to Roderick.

"I see," Roderick says flatly. He then bows to me and walks towards the main entrance doors.

"That was rude of him," Conrad complains. It takes all my patience and decorum training to not scream at him. Roderick Abbott is the better man. Not because he is the one my heart wants, but because he is the kinder of the two. I am not sure why Conrad has the personality and temperament he does when his family is very amicable.

Roderick has worked hard to attain the level of junior ambassador, and within the next year, he should have his own ambassadorship, making him the lead for our foreign affairs with one of our neighboring kingdoms. And with that rise in status also comes a raise in wage, meaning that he will soon have enough to take care of a wife and family. That thought causes my stomach to sour. Or it could be my present companion.

"Come along, Lord Ryan. My parents are waiting for me," I say to him, leaving him at the base of the stairs that lead to the private section of the royal palace.

Our castle is large—it has to be for a family of our size. It has two main sections: the private section for my family and the public section. The main entrance is between the two. Conrad huffs in irritation and storms off, walking much faster than my short legs will allow me to go. It's unfortunate that, as the eldest, I am also the shortest, except for the girls who are still growing.

As I reach the end of the entranceway, I see Roderick leave through the front doors. I want to run after him, but Father and Sabrina are standing near the door. Sabrina is waiting for me with her cloak on. Conrad bows to my parents before he leaves through the front doors.

"Are you looking forward to this evening?" Sabrina asks me as a footman aids me with my cloak. She smiles at me, her smile mirroring that of my four youngest sisters.

"Yes, mostly," I smile back at her.

Conrad's invitation was not a choice made by me or Sabrina. That disappointing decision belongs to my father. Together, the three of us walk through the front doors and to the carriage. Another footman helps me enter it, and after I sit, I arrange my gown and make myself comfortable. I want to be excited about tonight, but I am unsure how it will go because of the person I will sit next to all evening. Instead of dwelling on that, I look at my gown and smile.

Tonight, I am wearing one of my favorite gowns. The gown is a deep green, empire-waisted dress with cap sleeves adorned with embroidered flowers that encircle the sleeve and traverse the bodice. The lighter color of the thread disguises the flowers until closer inspection. I also love how the green matches my eyes—the same shade of green my father and sisters all have.

After the footman shuts the carriage door and we are on our way to the theater, Father finally speaks. I realize something is on his mind from the angry look on his face, but he did not want the staff to overhear. "Hazel, are you going to be this rude all evening?" Father demands of me.

"Father, I apologize!"

"No, but Lord Ryan seemed very upset as he left for his carriage tonight."

"I cannot see how that means I was rude, Father?" I ask him carefully.

Father does not see the 'Not now, dear' look that Sabrina is giving him. This is the first night out since she gave birth to my youngest sister, Rose, earlier this year.

"He was probably jealous of you speaking to Roderick," Father says.

"Wolf—" Sabrina starts, but Father waves a hand in her direction to stop.

"No, I am sure that is his problem. He was just jealous. You will take care to explain to him he has nothing to envy, won't you, Hazel?"

He might have says it like a question, but I know from the look on his face it was a command. How can my father expect me to do that, when it is Roderick I want to go on adventures with?

"And I think Conrad can balance you well."

Balance me well?

"What do you mean, Father?" I keep my tone polite, with effort.

"Well, it is just... you are so easily distracted. I know you try, but when you are queen, your husband will have to be more... solid." Father says, cringing at the words he has just spoken.

"I see," I breathe. Father believes I will not be a powerful queen on my own, but he still will not mention Gardenia inheriting the throne after him?

"Perhaps we can have this discussion tomorrow," Sabrina says. She doesn't like it when the family is upset and hopes to have a nice evening out. She rarely gets those as a mother of four young girls, stepmother of nine others, and queen of a kingdom. Being queen comes with many demands, not as many as what will be for me—or Gardenia—as that person will be the ruler and not the consort. But now I see Father expects me to take a role like Sabrina, not as the actual ruler.

After we arrive at the theater, Father exits the carriage first, then Sabrina. Before she places her hand in the footman's waiting outside for his help out of the carriage, she looks as if she wants to say something. But instead, she gives me a gentle smile and then exits the carriage.

I wonder about her thoughts, but if they are filled with pity, I don't want to hear them now. I take a deep breath and ready myself for a pleasant evening. Mostly agreeable. I still have to sit beside Conrad throughout the opera. The walk into the theater is short, and I am grateful, as tonight is an accurate representation of winter with its unusually cold temperatures. Verdant has mild winters, but there are always a few days that make it resemble our northern neighbor, Norland.

I am handing my cloak to a different footman when I hear my name. I look around and see Roderick. He smiles when he realizes I heard him say my name to the person he is talking to. He is only a few feet away from me in the theater's entryway, but the distance could be miles.

Apologizing, we both laugh. I nod at him to continue.

In his smooth voice, he apologizes for the interruption. It reminds me of the deep richness of coffee, like his brown eyes. The small fluttering in my stomach makes me think that butterflies have replaced the bats I felt earlier. "I wanted to give you something," he says and then hands me a small golden ball. I blink at the item as he places it in my hand.

"Thank you," I say to him with a smile. I am grateful he thought of me, but why did he think a ball would be a gift for me? He smiles back at me, then laughs. "What is so funny?" I ask him.

"You don't want to ask me about the reason I am giving you this ball, despite being confused."

I nod at him in response to his answer to my question. "Why did you give me a ball?" I ask him timidly.

"It is special; it can protect the one who has it from dark magic."

"Surely you need this more than I do with your travels?"

"I have a feeling you need it more than I do," he says earnestly. And with the look he is giving me, the fluttering butterflies take flight.

"This is very kind of you, Roderick. Thank you," I say quietly. He looks like he is about to say something more when he frowns at something behind me. Shaking his head slightly, he smiles and bows to me before walking away. I turn to find the reason for his quick departure and see that Sabrina is walking towards me with Conrad, with a slightly sour expression on her face. *Am I not alone in my dislike for Conrad?* I cannot help but wonder. I resist the urge to smirk.

"Are you ready to enjoy the opera?" Sabrina asks me in a gentle tone. I tuck the small golden ball into the pocket of my gown as I nod and smile at her. I take the arm she offers me, linking it with my own, and we make our way to our box in the theater. The thought of sitting next to Conrad all evening makes my stomach sour.

Thankfully, my unwanted companion did not ruin my evening at the opera. With her incredible performance, the soprano successfully stirred the emotions of the audience. The tale revolved around a woman's love for one man, but her family compelled her to marry someone wealthier, resulting in a beautiful yet tragic narrative. While trying to break up a fight between two men, the woman died. The eerie similarities this tale has to what I am feeling and facing is causing tears to well in my eyes. After the opera, mingling seems endless, with Conrad by my side. Different members of the court whisper when I walk past, with Conrad right beside me.

I am more than ready to go home by the time Sabrina says we are about to leave.

As she and I wait for our cloaks, Conrad says, "I will call on you tomorrow."

Before I can tell him, I will be busy, Sabrina kindly says, "I hope her schedule will allow time for a visit." Her face is smooth of any ill thoughts, but the spark in her eyes says to not challenge her. I am her wondering if she is the ally I thought her to be. I hope so because if I can work up the courage to tell her the truth, then I can do the same with my father. We receive our cloaks and link arms as we move to our carriage. When I turn around to see where my father is, he is still in a conversation, which means Sabrina and I will be alone in the carriage for a few minutes. Perhaps I can find the courage to tell her the truth, especially where Conrad is concerned.

We take our seats, and Sabrina asks, "You don't want to marry Conrad, do you?"

"Not particularly, no," I answer.

"Is there someone you would like to marry?"

"Yes." My answer is a whisper.

"Then why haven't you said anything, Hazel?" She is giving me a fierce look that says she cannot help me if she doesn't have all the information.

"Would it matter?" I look at her until she sighs and looks to the carriage door, which Father should enter through at any moment. Maybe this is my chance to bring up my desire to give up the throne, to let the kingdom pass to Gardenia. We each open our mouths to say something when the carriage door opens, and Father steps in. The moment slips away. I lose my chance.

"All going well, I hope?" he asks us both jovially. "It was an evening?"

"Yes, Father," I smile at him, because even being with Conrad, it was an evening.

"Of course, dear," Sabrina answers agreeably.

"Good, good," he replies with his eyes shining and a cheerful grin. I am glad that this evening was pleasant for my father. He deserves to have such moments.

And maybe tomorrow I can try again with Sabrina. Perhaps I can even use her as a buffer when Conrad calls.

Chapter Three
An Unforeseen Event

This morning's council meeting is going better than I could have expected. The golden ball Roderick gave me at the opera last night has been an invaluable aid throughout this boring meeting. I keep the ball in my hand or on my lap, and whenever I feel myself losing focus, I just spin the ball or squeeze it in my hand. Remarkably, I recall every detail of the meeting. As I sit across from Father in his office going over the meeting, he is smiling at me instead of frowning because I could answer all his questions.

Later this afternoon, when Conrad asks to meet with me, Sabrina comes to my rescue with my sisters in tow. We are in the family sitting room, and my sisters are all shining in their own unique ways. Azalea sketches, Marigold practices her singing, the twins practice their glares because of something Sabrina and Father told them at breakfast, and the youngest of my sisters play with their dolls at full volume. All of this noise prevents Conrad from having the intimate setting he, I'm sure, craves. Gardenia keeps Father occupied because Sabrina told us he wants to talk to Conrad after his visit.

I love my stepmother!

That is how the next few weeks go. The ball helps me through all of my tasks, and my interactions with Conrad are always busy with my sisters and stepmother. If I'm honest, I'm surprised my father hasn't caught on to our scheme. Conrad most definitely has. He is furious, if the stormy look he is giving me is an indicator. We are in the main entryway of the castle, so he can't do or say anything horrible with so many eyes to observe.

"Are you done hiding behind your insipid sisters?" he growls when he steps directly in my path. Maybe I am mistaken, and he is stupid enough to try something in public.

I raised my chin. "First, I am a princess and a lady; you should address me as such. Second, I do not appreciate what you are insinuating. You imply that the royal family is mistreating you when we have invited you into our home. Third, you are not a member of our family or my spouse; therefore, supervision is a must," I tell him sternly.

I must have been louder than I intended judging by the looks the guards and a few people coming and going in the public section of the castle are giving me. Conrad raises an eyebrow and looks like he is about to yell something when a familiar voice interjects.

"Perhaps we should move this conversation out of the main hall so the princess is not part of a spectacle," Roderick walks up to us, standing next to me. My heart skips a beat at his nearness. *No nervous sweats, please,* I command myself. This is the closest he has stood to me since the night he gave me the golden ball a few weeks earlier. I have wanted a moment alone with *him* every day, not Conrad. I nod my thanks to him, and we move to the hallway that leads to the steward's office.

Only one guard guards the steward's office, with no other staff members present. "You can go now, Abbott," Conrad says to Roderick with a superior tone.

"I am going to talk with my uncle's guard so I will be near," Roderick says to me and walks down the hallway. How could I have forgotten his uncle is my father's steward? That is how we met as children. He and the guard laugh at something, and the door opens, revealing his uncle, Oliver. Oliver waves Roderick into his office, and the guard follows, but they leave the door open, so I am not alone with Conrad.

"Why are you avoiding me?" Conrad asks in a charming voice, but when I meet his cold blue eyes, I sense a maliciousness in them.

"I am not avoiding you, Lord Ryan. I simply do not want my sisters' or my reputation ruined. Now, if you will excuse me, I have an appointment to get to," I tell him firmly but not unkindly. It is the truth. I have an appointment with Azalea in the Square Garden. She wants to do a series of small portraits of our sisters and the different gardens, and I'm going to be late if I do not get there in the next few minutes.

Gardens surround the castle. We have a circular garden, square garden, rock garden, statue garden, water garden, and a maze, among a few others. Gardening is a favorite pastime of Father's. It helps keep him centered and balanced, so he doesn't make any rash decisions. Of course, he still trains a little with his knights, but his relaxation time is in a garden.

I leave Conrad in front of the steward's office and make my way outside. I walk through the circular garden to get to the square one where Azalea is waiting. It's not quite spring, but today is warm enough that I do not need a heavy cloak. My long-sleeved dress will do. And I am happy to leave all thoughts of Conrad behind.

I hear footsteps behind me but think nothing of it. Verdant's citizens, who love the outdoors, have the privilege to visit the gardens during daylight hours. A few guards patrol the grounds, but we have never had a reason for any of us princesses to be trailed by a guard.

I am almost to the water garden, which is between the square and circular gardens, when someone grabs my arm. On instinct, I try to pull my arm free and see who has dared to grab me.

I see a furious Conrad. His nostrils are flaring, and eyes are bulging. His breathing is loud and fast. I have never seen him this angry; we have known each other since childhood thanks to his father being a duke. However, now I am genuinely afraid for the first time ever in his presence—not just apprehension or annoyance, but fear that he's going to hurt me. He was short-tempered as a child, but he never resorted to violence.

"What are you doing, Lord Ryan? Let go of me at once," I demand. He glares at me and sneers before saying, "No, you will stop and answer my questions so I can tell the king he has a man that will control you, that he need not look further for his true heir." Is this what he and my father have been discussing? Or is he so far gone into madness that he has misinterpreted my father's actions with my suitor selection?

"Control me? True heir? What lunacy are you speaking of? My father has thirteen daughters for heirs. One would be a fantastic queen, but that is not for anyone but my father to decide upon. I think you are confused, Lord Ryan."

My voice trembles, but I go on. "My father is not looking for an heir, but a strong male counterpart for his heir. You see, since Father has only daughters, he wants a marriage for all of us."

I pause and stare at his hand on my arm. He's applying such intense pressure to it, I'm certain it will cause a bruise, and I'm attempting to suppress my cries because of the pain.

I glare up at him. "You will not be an option because of this moment."

He blinks, then lets go of my arm. "That is your answer, then?" he growls quietly.

I nod at him. He nods in return and moves as if he is going to walk away, then suddenly turns back, pulling something out of his pocket. "So be it then," he snarls as he throws the object at me.

It all happens so fast, I have no time to react, but Roderick does. "No!" he cries and dives in front of me. Whatever Conrad threw hit Roderick with a small bang.

A cloud of red smoke bursts upward, and a splat hits the walkway stones.

"It was supposed to be you," Conrad yells with a red face and eyes that are cold. His legs are wide, and his breathing is faster before he runs away.

I am in shock. My mind unable to choose what to focus on—that Conrad tried to kill me or that Roderick saved my life at the cost of his own. Tears are now streaming from my eyes as I try to see through the smoke that is fading.

"Roderick!" I sob. "I'm so sorry."

"Why are you sorry?" his deep voice asks from inside the smoke.

"You... you're alive?" I ask, afraid to hope.

"Yes, so it seems." His tone sounds dry, almost sarcastic.

"I can't see you because of the smoke. Can you get up?"

"I'm not sure that is an idea, Hazel," he says flatly.

"Of course it is. I need to see that you are all right," I mumble.

The heavy stomp of guards' boots and clank of armor are rushing to my location. Maybe they can help Roderick with whatever Conrad has done. I can finally see more of the walkway and at least one guard rushing to me when something jumps at my face.

I scream and slap the large, slimy thing away with as much force as possible. It lands with a splat. This is not my finest moment.

"I told you," Roderick says, sounding like he is in pain or dazed.

The smoke finally clears, and I can see what has become of Roderick. Terror quickly replaces my relief because he is no longer a man.

He is now a frog.

"Princess, are you well?" the guard asks me while looking me over and checking our surroundings.

"I... I am," I mumble, but before I can finish, another guard arrives, almost stepping on Roderick.

"Don't hurt him!" I screech.

Both guards give me a curious look, but I stoop and pick up Roderick the frog, much to my shock, as I despise such creatures. They are disgusting—and why are they always covered in something gross?

"Sorry, Princess," the second guard says, sounding very confused. And who would blame him? He does not know what just happened. The poor man must be worried about me. And the look he is giving me as I hold Roderick the frog close to me is almost comical.

"We tried to get to you the moment we heard you scream, but there was a strange smoke that wouldn't let us pass through it." The first guard adds, "We didn't want to hurt you accidentally, Your Highness."

"I am well, but I need..." I am interrupted again, but this time by my father's booming voice asking where I am.

"Father, I am not hurt but I..." New sobs on Roderick's behalf overtake me.

"Come along, let's get you back to your room, and we can discuss what just happened," Father says soothingly as he wraps an arm around my shoulders.

Father's personal guards fall into step with us. I look over my shoulder and see the first two guards searching for something. Father tilts his head and raises his eyebrows. I am holding a frog after all.

I still hold on to Roderick as we walk through the hallways and stairways that lead to my room. Sabrina, Gardenia, and Azalea are all waiting for us inside. Seeing the relieved expression on their faces does me in again, and I sob anew.

Father rushes me to my chair, and my family tries to comfort me the best they can without comprehending what happened in the garden. When my tears have stopped, Azalea, being herself, asks in a gentle voice, "Is that a frog?"

I laugh unsteadily and nod, holding Roderick closer to me. *Why has he not said anything?*

"Can you tell us what happened now?" Father asks softly, "and in the straightest way possible." I guess years of being the daughter that daydreams, gets lost in thought, and loses track during a conversation has left its mark.

Blindly, I shift Roderick to my right hand and reach into my pocket for the golden ball with my left. I tell my family everything. When I get to the part where Roderick is the frog, he emits a croak and leaps from my hand to my lap, and then back again. I stop speaking and look at him. I think he is discreetly trying to shake his head no, but it is hard to tell with him as a frog.

"So, Conrad Ryan tried to curse the heir? My daughter?" Father asks with a menacing tone.

"Yes," I answer him quietly.

"I will take care of it," he says as he pats my shoulder and leaves my room in a hurry. Sabrina watches Father leave with pursed lips, and Gardenia is staring at Roderick the frog. Azalea walks to my private bathing room. She returns with a small bowl filled with water.

"I will fetch a stone from outside since you seem quite taken with this *frog*," Azalea says in her slow, soft voice and an arched eyebrow. Has she figured out the frog's identity? She places the bowl on the stand beside my bed. I blink at the bowl. It will have to be moved for reasons that I am not stating in front of my sisters and stepmother.

"You said Roderick was visiting Oliver, but he didn't come to find you when you left?" my Gardenia asks astutely. I am looking at my sister, debating on how to answer her when Roderick croaks and hops from my hand. He hops clumsily all the way to the bowl that Azalea got him. Once inside, he seems to be content, but Gardenia raises an eyebrow at my newfound *friend*.

"Yes," I say, also looking at Roderick, wondering if he will answer any of these questions himself. With a gentle tone, I quietly state, "I hope he is well." I hope he understands the sincerity behind every word. I won't rest until he's a man again.

Azalea leaves to go get the stone she mentioned. Nia looks at me like she wants to ask me something. A part of me wishes she would, but another part of me dreads her doing so.

Instead, she asks, "You are alright, aren't you?"

"I could be worse," I answer. She nods and gives a small smile in return.

"We will leave you to rest, Hazel," Sabrina says. "And if you want dinner in your room this evening, that will be perfectly fine."

"Thank you. I will let you know how I am faring later," I answer as she and Gardenia leave my room. While the door is still open, I see father has posted a guard outside my door, something that has never happened before. Conrad must still be missing.

I move from my chair to sit on my bed so I can privately talk to Roderick.

"Roderick?" I anxiously ask him and wait for a response.

CHAPTER FOUR

AN UNIMAGINABLE PROBLEM

I feel like I am waiting at sword point for his response.

"Hazel?" he finally says in his wonderful voice.

"What can I do to help you?"

"Knowing why Conrad planned this for you would be a start. I doubt he meant for you to remain a frog," he growls the last word. It is sadly comical hearing a frog growl. I shiver, looking at him, trying to contain my laughter. If a frog could give someone a glare, Roderick is attempting one with his grumpy expression.

"Is something about this situation humorous?"

"No," I answer him meekly.

"And yet you are trying not to laugh?"

"You growled," I whisper, and a small laugh eludes me.

He sighs. He almost rolls his eyes, but they do something weird, and the film covers them before he mutters, "I cannot stay angry with you."

"I don't want you to be angry with me," I whisper.

"We need to come up with some ideas to figure out how to change me back."

"Yes." I hesitate, and he blinks at me with the weird frog film eyes again. He doesn't say a word, so I continue, "Why did you not want me to say anything to my father or the rest of my family?"

"Perhaps we will, but I would like time to process and possibly fix this myself. I know it seems crazy, but I must try it my way first," he says imploringly.

"Fine, but we will need to come up with an explanation of where you have disappeared to and... figure out a few other things," I finish with a blush.

"I will not be sleeping in your room," he reassures me.

"Agreed," I mumble, and my face flames even more. "Perhaps I can place you in my bathing room or in the sitting room my sisters and I share."

He thinks for a moment, and I look about my room to give him the semblance of privacy.

"I think the sitting room will do well, but I would like to join you for meals and some of your daily tasks."

"Okay," I say, more than a little confused by his request.

"Thank you, Hazel. I appreciate your help with this."

"You appreciate my help?" I gaze at him. "It's my fault you are a frog!" I exclaim, with new tears welling up.

"No, it is Conrad's fault," Roderick says darkly.

And then I remember Roderick gave me the golden ball that I still have clutched in my hand. He gave it to me for protection. I hold it up and ask, "Did you not trust the ball to work? Did you think it wouldn't protect me?" I ask with a hiccup from my crying.

"I didn't think about it," he mumbles. Even quieter still, he adds, "I reacted on instinct."

I take a few deep breaths to calm myself and process what he has said.

"On instinct?" I ask.

This is the most honest and intimate conversation I have ever had with someone who is not a member of my family. I am thrilled and terrified all at once. He shifts a little in the bowl, which I recognize as something I use for my hair ornaments.

Good thinking, Azalea. I doubt I would have thought of something to use that fast. It clearly shows how creative she is. While Roderick surveys his surroundings, I do the same in my room. I don't feel embarrassed that he is seeing my room, my sanctuary, although I probably should. I know his being in here is technically inappropriate, as he is a man... regardless of his current resemblance to a frog.

He finally answers. "I reacted on the instinct that tells me to protect you, guard you. It was the same instinct that told me to give you the golden ball." Our eyes met, and if he wasn't a frog, I would kiss him.

Where did that thought come from?

I cannot kiss a frog for a multitude of reasons, but mainly because I want my first kiss to be with Roderick the man, not Roderick the frog. We are sitting in companionable silence when Azalea knocks on my door. She enters with a maid following behind her, carrying a small tea service and a few snacks on the tray.

"I have the stone for the bowl," Azalea says as she walks across my room. Before she puts it in the water, she shows it to Roderick, as if asking if it meets his approval. When he swims to one side, she places the smooth stone near the opposite edge.

"This way, he can come and go out of the bowl as he pleases without making a mess," Azalea says.

"Thank you for your help, Azalea," I smile at my sister.

"Are you going to join us for dinner this evening?" She asks me the question, but she is clearly fixated on Roderick.

"Yes, and I'll be bringing him along, too." I smirk at her. She gives me the mischievous grin we all inherited from our mother and says, "Good." Without another word, she turns and leaves my room, with the maid following right behind her. The maid had set up the tea and snacks on the table beside the chair closest to the fireplace. I'm wondering if it will be safe to move Roderick over there when he speaks.

"I knew I liked her."

"What do you mean?" I ask, confused.

"She knows," he says with meaning.

Roderick is right. Azalea might be the quietest of us all, but she is the most observant. She has to be, with the talents she has with painting, sketching, and her other artistic hobbies.

"Are you all right with that?" I cautiously ask him.

"Of course. She's the least likely of your sisters to cause problems with this knowledge."

"What do you mean by that?" I ask him in a defensive tone.

"I have no siblings, but I have a few cousins. And I have been around the royal family long enough to know that you, Gardenia, and Marigold would do your best to help but would most likely say something to your father before I am ready for him to know. The twins are gossips, and while you all are full of good intentions, you most likely would get distracted and lose focus. Azalea is the one that sees and hears more than the rest of you but never says or does anything with the information." He speaks smoothly and, sadly, full of truth.

"You really know us so well."

"Yes," he says shyly.

I don't want to cause him any embarrassment, so I ask if he would like to see the snacks Azalea prepared. She is authentically thoughtful. The tray has raisins, blueberries, and some peas, all small and easy for me—or a frog—to eat. She also includes a bit of roasted chicken, but she has stripped it from the bone and shredded it. For most of the afternoon, Roderick and I experiment with different foods to see what he can eat as he gets used to his new form. Apparently, it is not a natural talent for one to hop across a room, especially when that person has been used to walking for over two decades.

When I pictured spending time alone with Roderick, I can't say this is what I envisioned, but I love it all the same because it's just the two of us.

And there's a muted pleasantness with him, no matter his form.

CHAPTER FIVE

A CURIOUS DILEMMA

Dinner tonight became a subdued affair. It might not be the custom with all royal families, but with one as large as ours, I appreciate that even my youngest sister is here, and she is not yet one. However, the younger girls are too eager by Roderick's frog form to stay seated. The twins, at thirteen, kept rolling their eyes and snickering at our sisters, younger than them. The middle girls, who are the daughters from Father's second wife, and Sabrina's girls are being sent back to the nursery or their rooms with their maids and nurses. I don't blame the younger girls. For them, dinner with all of us typically boring, all at the dinner table, was an exciting thing when a frog is present. So now, it's just the four eldest of the thirteen daughters remaining at the table with Father and Sabrina.

Father glares at Roderick for a portion of the evening, but he can tell having the frog near helps me feel better. When I leave dinner, I have two armed guards escorting me to my room. Someone will stay outside my room until

Conrad is caught. During dinner, Father told us he had Conrad's parents questioned, and he believes them to be innocent of his crimes. I am glad for their sakes and for the sake of Conrad's sister, for she is a sweet girl who is between Marigold's and the twins' age. Because when they apprehend him, the court will probably ostracize them and strip them of their dukedom.

Father has multiple knights investigating where Conrad could have purchased whatever he used to curse me. Our cousin Jacob kindly volunteered to be an investigator as well. Growing up, Jacob was like a brother to us older girls, but after Father's brother, Jacob's father, died a few years ago, our cousin became a Duke at 16 years old and has been too busy to spend much time with us,

I place the bowl for Roderick on a tall shelf in the sitting room all of us girls share, but he wants to talk before going to bed, so I carry him into my room and set him on the other chair. Two comfortable armchairs sit beside my fireplace. I am not sure if my room can be considered large, but I am very fortunate to have such a beautiful room and belongings. Positioned across the room from the fireplace is a small writing desk and chair, with my bed in the center of the room, thankfully protected by curtains for privacy. I am not sure if I am comfortable with Roderick seeing where I sleep.

I wait for a moment after sitting in my chair to see if he will start the conversation. When he just sits on the chair looking at me, my anxiety builds, and I feel like I need to force myself to face him. *You can do this, Hazel. You two have been friends for years.* With a deep breath and a mental shake, I ask him, "What did you want to discuss?"

"I am rethinking that now, if I am honest. Before I bring up that subject, I would like to see how tomorrow goes," he says coolly. I wince at his short tone.

"All right. Do you want me to carry you back to the bowl in the sitting room?" I ask him softly. My chest tightens, and I can feel myself blushing in embarrassment.

"If you would be so kind as to do so," he replies. "Hazel, I want to apologize for hurting you a moment ago, but I want to think over my words more."

I pick him up and gently carry him to the sitting room. After tossing and turning for what feels like forever, I finally fall asleep with dreams of red smoke, bangs, and splats.

I take breakfast in my room the next day. With the little and restless sleep I had gotten, I need more time to prepare myself for the day ahead. I save some of my breakfast for Roderick. While my maid, who I share with Gardenia, fixes my hair in another updo, he eats it, and I find it amusing to see the comical expressions she gives Roderick.

The maid takes the small plate from my breakfast when she leaves, still giving Roderick a curious look. I like her, but I would say she's closer to Gardenia than me. Not that I mind; my closest friend is currently a frog, so I'm trying to deal with that.

"Are you ready to see how I spend my day?" I ask Roderick.

"Yes, I'm curious how you see the council meetings," he says in that familiar, smooth voice of his. It is so odd to see a frog; a large green frog that has spots and bumps that might be warts all over his body. I resist the urge to shiver. The only reason I could carry him yesterday is because of the shock and newness of the situation—at least, that is what I keep telling myself.

"Is there a problem, Princess?" Roderick asks, sounding amused.

"Umm, no," I stammer. I moved to pick him up, and he jumped at me. I don't believe I should be the one to blame for what happened next.

As I step forward with my hands raised, Roderick jumps, and I instinctively react. I smack him so hard he flies across the room, and I shriek. In this form, which had been meant for me, I would have given Conrad anything to be human again.

At my terrified scream, the guard posted outside my room bursts in with his sword raised, causing another scream to erupt from me. But closely behind the guard are three of my sisters—Gardenia, Marigold, and Azalea—all peeking around him, making sure I am well.

The expressions on my three sisters' faces and the perplexed one on the guard's face as he scans for the threat that caused me to scream leads me to laugh. The splat sound when Roderick hit the stones of my floor did not help the situation, but the faces of the four people staring at me sent me into a fit of giggles. Feeling a little bad for leaving him on the floor, I force myself to pick him up.

"Sorry, he jumped at me, and I wasn't expecting it," I tell the guard and my sisters. I try not to snicker at my reaction to a frog jumping at me, but soon, the poor guard finds himself outnumbered by four laughing princesses.

"Are you sure there is nothing wrong, Princess?" the guard asks me, sounding put out by being assigned to my protection detail. Roderick voices his opinion with a boisterous croak. The guard shakes his head and goes back to standing outside my door in the hallway. He shuts my door, resuming his post. My sisters waste no time asking questions, each speaking over each other.

"Did Conrad really try to curse you?"

"Why didn't the curse work?"

"Have you heard about Roderick?"

Gardenia asks the last question, and I give her a look of confusion. I remember she doesn't know he is a frog and is here, but she knows of my feelings for him, so I ask, "What?"

Gardenia answers, "No one has seen him since he left his uncle's office yesterday," she says calmly and in a neutral tone. She's expecting a reaction from me, and I belatedly remember that I need to pretend I do not know what happened to him. He's a frog. He's currently sitting in my hands.

"No one has seen him?" I ask, trying to give Roderick time to make his choice whether to reveal himself to all three of my sisters. I look at him pointedly. He looks back at me, but I cannot read his expression. He blinks in that weird sideways blink frogs do, and I almost drop him. He's sticky and heavy, not at all attractive.

Which is unfortunate because I like Roderick's face. It is handsome and pleasing. His brown eyes, smooth and rich like coffee, are filled with kindness. Roderick's hair is a sandy color, and he has a tan from his travels. And his smile can chase away any fear or doubt.

"Or have *certain people* seen him?" Nia asks me directly. I see the frown on her face and the dark look in her eyes.

"I spent the night in your sitting room, so I know Azalea did not say a word," Roderick says to me, and Nia and Mari both look shocked. "You are very astute, Princess Gardenia," he says. He keeps his voice calm, but he shifts in my hands as if he is nervous.

Azalea smiles and moves to take one of my chairs. She has a weaker constitution than most of us, so she must rest often. "I knew it," she whispers with a smirk.

"How did you know?" Marigold asks before biting her lip.

"It was really quite easy to figure out," Azalea says. She takes a moment to continue, which means this is a tough morning for her. "Roderick looks at Hazel the way she looks at him when they think no one is around or watching. Also, I heard his scream when Conrad threw whatever he did at Hazel. I'm honestly surprised no one else has figured it out. If Roderick was really missing, Hazel would lead the search party."

Roderick laughs. I giggle, but I hadn't realized anyone other than Gardenia knew of my feelings. I have also never caught Roderick looking at me the way Azalea says he has.

"Perhaps we should leave certain parts of the conversation to Hazel and Roderick alone," Gardenia suggests with a wink.

"Thank you, Princess," Roderick says, with what might be a frog's version of a smile, and "How did you know?" he asks Gardenia.

"Hazel doesn't like frogs," she answers him plainly.

"That is true," I tell him. "If I had become a frog, Conrad could have asked me for anything, and I would have given him whatever he wanted if he would change me back." I turn away from the accusing looks on Roderick's and Gardenia's faces. I look around my room because my other two sisters also smirk and are interpreting Roderick's look correctly.

"But how did Conrad know I don't like frogs?"

"You don't remember the incident in the water garden?" Marigold asks me. The confusion must be evident on my face, because she continues, "A frog jumped onto the path in front of you while you were taking a stroll during a garden party," she says, refreshing my memory. I remember because it scared me. I shrieked when it landed in front and I tried to run away, but I couldn't because my parents had given Conrad permission to escort me for a stroll through the water garden, and he wouldn't let go of my hand.

"Oh," I say, filled with embarrassment. I shift Roderick to a more comfortable position in my hands. He's not exactly a lightweight frog.

"Yes, many of the guests learned of your aversion then," Gardenia says.

"I see," I mutter.

"My question is, how did he buy a curse?" Roderick says, a little irritated. "He is not a mage, and I do not believe there is one in the Ryan family, so how was he able to turn me into a frog?"

"I am not sure," I tell him truthfully, "but if you want, I can try to look into curses after the council meeting, unless you want me to tell Father what has happened to you?" I ask.

"No, thank you," he says stiffly. "I might be a frog at the moment, but the fewer who know of my humiliation, the better."

"Marigold and I can start looking into mages in the library while you three attend the meeting," Azalea says quietly. "It will be suspicious if you and Gardenia both miss the meeting, and Roderick is entitled to whatever privacy we can give him."

"True," Gardenia says, but the way she bites her lip, I know something is bothering her.

"What is it?" I ask Gardenia.

"If revealing your secret will save or stop something worse from happening, then I will tell Father," she says, looking at Roderick.

"I agree," he says after a moment. "I do not want any harm to befall any of you. If keeping my secret will do more harm than good, then please inform His Majesty of my dilemma."

"Thank you," Gardenia says, with a sigh of gratitude. "We should go, or we will be late to the meeting." She heads for my door, and I follow her with Roderick. Marigold and Azalea join us in the hall after a moment. We all walk together until we reach the public section. Gardenia and I walk into the council meeting room where chaos is reigning.

CHAPTER SIX

AN OBSERVATION OF DUTY

I tentatively enter the council room. The council members are all red in the face, yelling at each other. These men all sound like what I imagine a battle to sound like, loud and confusing. Father is sitting in his chair at the head of the room, and he is furious at what is currently happening. The guard with me looks at the chaotic scene in front of us, sees no immediate danger to me, and steps back into the hallway, shutting the door after he exits.

I glance down at Roderick and question the wisdom of him being here with me. Gardenia fidgets next to me. I wish I were back in my room avoiding this situation.

I look at my sister, unsure what to do. She is concentrating on what the council members are yelling. A quick glance at Roderick shows he is listening too. I walk farther toward my desk at the back of the room with Gardenia right behind me. Knowing I shouldn't leave Gardenia alone to discover what caused this ruckus, I pay attention to their loud voices.

"Why is a duke's son being hunted?"

"Where is the steward's nephew?"

"Are all of us in danger from an evil mage?"

Wait, some of these people are angry because Conrad is being hunted, just because he is a duke's son? *Those who do evil things come in all shapes, sizes, and classes.* Conrad shouldn't get any more or less of a punishment because of his class. Father sees us before we take our seats, and I cannot tell if he is happy or angry that we are there. I set Roderick on my desk, and Father frowns at him. I take my seat, and Gardenia grabs her own.

"Enough!" Father says firmly, with a volume I rarely hear him use. "If you cannot act and speak in a civilized manner, then leave!" As his daughter, I am familiar with his tone. He's run out of patience, and the council members better pay attention.

They swiftly sit down. A few continue their arguments for a moment until they see Father's face.

"Yesterday, Conrad Ryan attacked my daughter. His family does not know of his dealings or where he could be hiding. Around the same time Conrad tried to injure my daughter, Junior Ambassador Abbott went missing. Shortly before both events took place, my daughter and

Conrad had a heated public discussion that was interrupted by Junior Ambassador Abbott."

At that, Father takes a deep breath and looks around the room. Then he looks at me with the golden ball clutched in my hand and a frog on my desk. Father subtly shakes his head at me, and his cheek twitches, meaning he was trying not to smile at me and my ridiculous companion. I have received that look more than once in my life.

"My gracious king," Oliver, his steward, begins once the room falls silent. "We are all glad that your daughter is safe and well, but what actions have been taken to find my nephew?"

Roderick visibly fidgets, but he opts to remain silent about being cursed, and I will honor his decision despite my disagreement.

"We have guards and knights looking for both young men," my father says gravely. "I do not believe Roderick would do anything to hurt my daughter, but his disappearance, simultaneous with Conrad's, is very suspicious."

I see Gardenia shift her head to look at me from the corner of my eye. As badly as I want to react, I cannot. If I were to say anything, it would hurt Roderick, and he jumped in front of a curse for me. I already passionately care for Roderick, and now I owe him.

The meeting continues, talking about both young men at first and eventually moving on to other topics that need to be addressed. The golden ball helps, but I feel my gaze going to Roderick more than once. Father must have noticed too, because I catch him shaking his head and looking at me as I am picking up Roderick.

After this council meeting, I must attend a few events that could not be rescheduled. The first is a tea for the young ladies at court. Gardenia may attend this with me, as a young lady of marriageable age. We all quietly sip our drinks and focus most of our conversations on Roderick and Conrad and where they might be, which makes me uncomfortable. I try to change the conversation to other things, so does Gardenia, but the ladies only want to speak of the two young men. Halfway through the tea, Roderick caught the attention of everyone present by jumping into a bowl of punch. Their shocked cries and his eyes peeking above the liquid had me giggling.

I refuse to cancel the second event as it involved the city's orphanage. As long as the weather permits, the children of the orphanage are getting a private tour of some of the royal family's gardens and as it is a very nice day, the tour goes on as planned. But I keep daydreaming about ways to help Roderick and what life might be like when he's a man again. I notice that throughout the day, I am never alone with Roderick; one of my sisters who knows our situation chaperones us constantly. They aren't being nosy or pushy, just making sure that everything is proper and respectful. I find it endearing, honestly.

The day is long and, by the time I return to my room, I am exhausted. Gardenia is in my room with Roderick and me, while the evening guard is outside my door. I take my favorite chair and place the bowl with fresh water for Roderick on the table next to me. Gardenia sits at my desk; she is being a dutiful chaperone but also making some notes to go over with Father.

"There are a few things I would like to discuss with you, Princess," Roderick says after hopping out of his bowl. His tone is serious, causing my stomach to turn and I reach for the golden ball in my pocket. Not knowing what he wants to talk about makes me anxious.

But this is Roderick, and I don't have an actual reason to be afraid. "What do you want to talk about?" I murmur to him.

"You do not enjoy your tasks as the heir, do you?" he asks me pointedly.

"I'm sorry?" I ask sharply.

"Hazel, I'm going to be honest with you," he says. If I'm reading his expression correctly, he is uncomfortable, but it's hard to tell. "For years, I could tell you wanted a different life. You might not remember, but before I started on my tour as a junior ambassador, we would talk. As friends, we asked each other what kind of future we envisioned for ourselves. We both wanted to travel, to see the beauties and wonders of the Creator's creation. But I noticed after you turned eighteen, you changed. Despite attempting to force yourself into that role, you never aspired to be the heir. You wanted to go on adventures. You aspired to be of use to Verdant, but not rule it. So, what happened?"

I blink at him because I remember those conversations. We would be at social events, and since I didn't have to choose a suitor, I could spend time with my friend. The friend who I imagined as my partner in all of my adventures. But I don't know if I can answer him. I am afraid of the truth; it will hurt my father and possibly my sisters. How can I tell him I want to leave this all behind and try an adventure?

"You didn't want to hurt anyone," he guesses by my silence.

"That," I say in a whisper, "and I am afraid. It is one thing for me to dream about going on adventures when, in reality, my responsibilities come with obligations—obligations it wouldn't be fair to pass off on to someone else, especially someone who never asked for it."

"I see," he says dejectedly. He slumps. It isn't just my heart I've broken, but his as well.

"It doesn't have to be that way," Gardenia says quietly. I hadn't noticed her come across the room. Roderick shifts to face her as she takes the other chair. " I believe you try your best, but you would be miserable as queen, and I don't want that for you." She hesitates, and with a sigh finally says, "I know what you have given up, and even though I think you would make a great queen., but you would be miserable." Shifting in her seat, she displays her discomfort with what she has said. She speaks a truth that will be met with disapproval by many. One that our father will not see.

"So, you see it too?" Roderick asks her.

"What do you mean?" I ask them both.

"I think he means how you struggle," Gardenia says softly. Though I almost didn't catch what she said. I stare at her, puzzled. She gives me a crooked grin before saying, "Hazel, you hate sitting in the council meetings. It is normal to get bored every once in a while, to even daydream occasionally. But with the duties of the heir, you struggle. You struggle to pay attention. You struggle to complete tasks. It's because your heart's not in it."

"Oh," I say shakily. I am feeling so many emotions after hearing what my sister had to say: shock, hurt, confusion, and joy. Shock that others have seen my struggles. Hurt that I am not truly the best for the job. Confusion because I am realizing I am not alone in this. And joy. I choose to focus on the joy because it confirms what I think, and about what Roderick has said as well. He, too, knows what I have been feeling.

"What do I do?" I ask them. "How do I tell Father that I want to help Verdant, but in a different way?"

"Have you thought about what this means for you, for any children you may have?" Roderick asks.

I know what Roderick is getting at. If I ask to not be the heir, I must officially petition to be removed from the line of succession. Any children I have will also be removed from the line of succession. But I have thought of this, and I think it is possible to raise children to appreciate their life and not be angry about things they cannot control. My children would still have titles, but not a seat on the throne.

"I have thought about it, and I am happy to give up the throne. And it is possible to have children and raise them to be happy and content with a life without a throne," I answer him sincerely.

"Truly?" Roderick asks me hopefully.

"Truly," I say. I look down at my lap as I feel heat envelop my face in a blush. Gardenia smiles at me, and Roderick hops into his bowl. I think the human emotions and the fire going in the fireplace are making him warm. Watching him get comfortable makes my sister grin, and a tiny smirk graces my face as well.

Gardenia suggests we say goodnight and stands up from her chair. "I can place you back in the sitting room if you'd like," she asks Roderick.

Roderick replies, "I would appreciate that, thank you."

As she picks up Roderick's bowl and starts walking to the door, she whispers, "Goodnight, sister."

"Goodnight, sister, Roderick." I rise from my chair and pull the sash that will let my maid know I am ready for her to help me get ready for bed.

"Goodnight, Hazel," Roderick says before Nia walks through the door. Even with everything going on, peace fills me after the conversation with Gardenia and Roderick.

I sleep well until a guard rushes into my room. My father needs to see me at once. The sun hasn't even risen.

Chapter Seven

A Truth Revealed

The guard does not give me much time, so I grab a robe and knock on Gardenia's door. The guard gives me an impatient glare, but I want my sister with me. Once Gardenia opens her door and I explain Father has summoned me, she rushes to grab her own robe. It is a quick march from our rooms to Father's office. Why am I being rushed through the castle as quickly as my short legs will carry me? Many dark thoughts are going through my mind. Is there something wrong with Father or Sabrina?

When we reach Father's office, the guard stops and waits for two other guards to open the door and let Gardenia and me in. Father is behind his desk. A few guards in front of him are pointing their swords at a man bound between them.

"Come in, Hazel," Father commands. He raises an eyebrow at us. "Gardenia. Girls, please stand over here." Father indicates to the side of his desk, away from the man that is bound in chains. Once we are in place, I look from Father to the man in chains.

Even with his head drooped, I can tell it's Conrad. At my gasp, Gardenia grabs my hand.

"I wish I did not need to bother you with this, but he has said little other than he wants to speak with the Princess," Father informs us darkly.

"What do you need to say, Conrad?" My voice shakes from nerves. I can't fathom what he could have to say to me, but I will hear it and then have nothing to do with him.

"It was supposed to be you," Conrad says quietly.

"What was supposed to be her?" Father demands. Conrad doesn't say a word. He lifts his head and glares at me. I am finally feeling more awake.

"He means the attack was intended for me," I say, my voice small and quivering with my anxiety and fear.

"What?" Father asks me, confused. "Was there something more than just the red smoke the guards couldn't get through?"

I say louder, "The curse was meant for me."

"It was!" Conrad yells. Gardenia and I both jump at Conrad's shout. I'm not sure who squeezed whose hand first, but having my sister with me helps and gives me strength.

"What curse?" Father asks, sounding equal measures of exasperation and anger.

"The one I bought for her," Conrad growls. He tries to break from the guards, and they almost impale him with their swords for his effort. "I was promised," he hisses. "She is supposed to be mine."

The room is silent after his last words. I can hear my heartbeat in my ears and not much else.

"What does he mean when he says I was supposed to be his?"

"What do you mean, she is supposed to be yours?" Father asks, each word dark and pointed. If Father were a mage, I am sure he would have frozen Conrad with his glare.

"You all but said she was mine, and when I couldn't get her to change her mind, I got a backup method," Conrad snarls at Father. "I spent more gold on you than you're worth," he spits in my direction.

Gardenia pulls me backward, and when I look at her face, I'm a little surprised at what I see. Her face is void of any emotion. She isn't giving Conrad a childish glare; she's giving him the look of a disgusted queen. I look over at Father. He seems confused by what he sees in her. Maybe he will finally see what I have for years.

Maybe this will be my chance to tell Father the truth, if only I can find the courage.

I want to say something to Conrad, but he continues, "You made it so easy to know how to win against you, Princess," he snarls. " If Roderick hadn't interfered, you would already be mine."

"So glad somebody finally remembered me," Roderick wheezes from the doorway. He had hopped across the castle to get here. Releasing Gardenia's hand, I make my way towards where he is resting in front of the door. I still want to gag at his frog form, but I pick him up anyway.

"I'm sorry, Roderick. I needed Gardenia with me." Despite my hesitation, my guilt cannot only be clear on my face. "I forgot about you. I am so sorry."

Roderick, sounding more like himself, says, "You are forgiven." I walk back over to where Gardenia is waiting, and Roderick adds, "You were awakened in a terrifying manner. I understand why you wanted your sister and could not think of anyone else."

"Roderick?" Father asks, sounding shocked.

"I am here, Your Majesty." Roderick tries to bow in my hands and almost rolls out of them. "I am alive, but I don't know if I would say I am well." He sounds like the confident man who has advanced rapidly in the ranks of the diplomacy department for Verdant.

"How... what?" Father asks, sounding angry. He turns towards Conrad. "You meant to turn Hazel into a frog?" Father asks him incredulously.

"Would you have given me everything I wanted if the spell had hit you?" Conrad asks me.

I take a deep breath, straighten my shoulders, and answer with sincerity, sadness. "Yes, I would have." Glancing down at Roderick, I hope he recalls our conversation from a few hours ago. "I truly dislike frogs. I would have given up everything to not be one."

Conrad smiles, and the maliciousness I saw in his eyes yesterday is clear for everyone in the room to see.

Father shocks everyone in the room with his reaction. A full body shaking laugh. I stare at him, bewildered. Gardenia has smoothed her face into a calm, blank expression. I wish I could do that, but that is a thought for a different moment.

"Father?" I ask tentatively. Roderick shifts in my hands to get a better look at his king. Father sits at his desk and calms himself before speaking.

"You wanted to turn Hazel into a frog so she would marry you?" he asks Conrad.

"Yes," Conrad answers him petulantly.

Father taps a finger on the desk. "How is the spell or curse undone?"

Conrad is silent for a moment, but Father stares at him until he finally breaks and starts talking again.

"A kiss," he whines. When everyone continues to stare at him, he adds, "My kiss was supposed to break the curse."

"I will remain a frog, thank you very much, sir."

Sadly, all heard the snort that escapes me.

"I doubt a kiss from me would work," Conrad replies to Roderick darkly.

"What do you mean by that?" Gardenia asks him. "Wasn't it designed for you to break the curse?"

"Not entirely," he mumbles.

"Explain," Gardenia demands.

"It was a standard spell. I specified the animal and the requirement for breaking it," Conrad explains. Everyone again stares at him, irritated by his lack of forthcoming information. "It wasn't a true love kiss spell, it was just a kiss requirement to undo it," he mumbles.

"Interesting," she says calmly. "Hazel, a kiss from you should work then."

"What?" I squeak and almost drop Roderick, trying to keep him in my hands. When I squeeze him, he cries out in pain. "I'm sorry," I say. With a perplexed expression, I gaze at my sister as if she has gone mad. "I cannot just kiss him."

"Why not?" Roderick and Gardenia both ask. I set him on Father's desk and look at him, then at my sister, confused. She's still blank-faced, but I know that gleam in her eye; she believes this will help me.

"It isn't proper," I answer them both.

"Ha!" Conrad erupts into a fit of hysterical laughter. "She doesn't want you, Abbott, because you're a frog!" The two guards holding his chain restraints look very amused with their charge.

"That's not..." I hesitate to continue because I am unsure how to explain why I do not want to kiss Roderick in a room for all people. What if it doesn't work? Why must we have an audience for a kiss?

"Hazel," Roderick says calmly. I gaze at him, and he reassures me in his soothing voice, saying, "Everything is fine."

The reassurance he is offering me is so loving, it breaks my heart again. He understands how this is making me feel, and a tear falls from my eye.

"Father, can we finish questioning Conrad later?" Gardenia asks him, not unkindly. She was firm but not rude, showing him again this side I knew she had. *Maybe that conversation helped her as well.*

"Yes," Father says, then nods to the guards. "Have the captain alert me to whatever your investigation finds."

Conrad's guards each grab an arm and begin escorting him out of Father's office. Before he is through the door, he yells, "She will never kiss you! You'll never be consort!"

"I never thought I would be," Roderick says quietly, earning looks from Father, Gardenia, and me. When he notices he has all of our attention, he says, "That doesn't matter now. About that kiss, please do not feel uncomfortable or obligated."

"Obligated?" Father asks.

"He jumped in front of me, taking the spell that Conrad meant for me," I answer him, "but I do not feel obligated. I just did not want a large audience, especially since we don't know if this will work."

"I see," Father says, and when I look at him, it is obvious he is uncomfortable with the thought of his daughter kissing.

"Allow me to offer a small suggestion," Gardenia says. Father nods at her, and she says, "What if you step into the hall or the council room, and I move over by the window? That will give them privacy but also keep things proper."

Father frowns but does what Gardenia suggests and walks into the council room; his guard follows him. Gardenia moves to the opposite side of the room and stands by the window. I adjust Father's chair so that the back angles towards Gardenia, affording Roderick and me more privacy.

"I meant what I said," Roderick says in between hops across Father's desk. "There's no need for you to do this. You don't have to kiss me."

I clarify, "It's not because of how I feel about frogs that I hesitate to kiss you." The moisture growing in my hands is becoming palpable. I rub them across my robe to remove the sweat that has formed there. "What if this doesn't work?" I ask him softly.

"Then I, most unwillingly and definitely uncomfortably, will accept a kiss from Conrad and hate myself throughout the entire experience," he says jokingly.

"Really?"

"Really," he replies calmly.

"Alright," I sigh. Before I can talk myself out of it or feel grossed out at having a frog this close to my face and mouth, I lean forward and kiss the top of his head. Red smoke and a bang cause me to jump backwards, and I almost hit Father's chair.

"Roderick?" I ask cautiously.

Gardenia's voice has a hint of fear as she asks if I am well, and I can hear Father and his guards mumble about the smoke as they enter the room again.

"I am well, but I am not sure about Roderick," I answer Gardenia.

"Ugh," Roderick grumbles. "I think it worked. And I desperately want a hot bath. I feel awful."

"It did?" I ask excitedly. As I stand up from the chair, the red smoke prevents me from seeing in front of me. I collide with a solid, warm wall—not a wall, but a body. I feel a blush building. Roderick is not a scrawny man, but a lean, muscular one. And I just crashed into him.

"It worked!" I shout with joy and jump to throw my arms around his shoulders. It is an impulsive reaction, but he wraps his arms around me, too. We stand like that for a little while until the smoke clears, and Father exclaims, "Remove your arms from around my daughter and move apart."

But I laugh, and Roderick joins me. Gardenia is trying her best not to smile.

"It is too early for this conversation," Father says with a tired expression. "We can all meet later today. I am glad you are back, Junior Ambassador Abbott. I believe you and I have much to discuss." Father gives him a stern look. Roderick nods.

"Thank you," he says to me and leaves Father's office.

"So, he is your choice for consort?" Father asks me. I step around his desk to give myself a moment. This is it.

I can tell him. I can stand in front of him and express my true feelings. Gardenia joins me; she links arms with mine. I look at her, and she gives me an encouraging grin and a brief nod of silent encouragement.

"No," I say quietly. Father gives me a confused expression. With a deep breath, I muster up the courage to continue in a louder but still nervous tone. "I am not choosing him as consort because I do not aspire to be queen. I think Gardenia would be the better option."

"It's just nerves; we all feel that from time to time." Father smiles.

"No, Father. I want to travel. I want to help Verdant but not as queen. Do you know what I've dreamed of for years?" I ask him. Tears fall from the mix of emotions I am feeling—anxiety, fear, hope, and relief. Father takes his chair and rubs his hand down his face. Perhaps I should not have said this now. Maybe this should have waited until later. No, if I wait, I will lose my courage.

Father sighs, and it sounds sad. "I knew you wanted to travel, but I thought you had outgrown it because you have said nothing about it in years."

"The person I shared my adventure plans with the most was gone on his own adventures, and you asked me to pick up more responsibilities. I struggled with them and knew I was disappointing you. I didn't want to make it worse, so I stopped talking about it."

"Roderick?" Father asks me.

"From our childhood, we have been and still are close. We both talked about being ambassadors for Verdant. It was expected for me to be queen, but you have almost always had Gardenia trained too. I thought you knew how I felt. Then Roderick began his training and left, and you increased my duties as the heir. I am grateful that you allowed Nia to join me on some tasks because if there is one daughter who is meant to be the next queen of Verdant, it is her."

"Do you understand what not being the heir and queen means for you and your descendants?" Father asks as his voice cracks in sadness. He furrows his brow and rubs his temples as if he is getting a headache.

"I do. If they take me out of the line of succession, I, as well as any children I have, will also be removed from that line. But I know it is possible to raise children to be content with their lot in life, thanks to you and Sabrina."

He looks at me for a moment, then at Gardenia. There is more to discuss, but we can postpone it. "I'll have Oliver notify the council there will be no morning meeting, thanks to both men being returned. I want to continue this conversation after each of us has rested."

"Yes, Father," Gardenia and I both say. We say good-night to Father, even though it is early morning, and depart to our rooms. My emotions have left me in a state of complete confusion. I kissed Roderick, turning him back into a man. I spoke the truth to Father, and he doesn't seem to hate me for it, which is an immense relief after revealing my feelings.

In the hallway, she links her arm with mine and leans in close, whispering in my ear, "You did it."

EPILOGUE

A FULFILLED WISH

It has been six months since I signed the documents to no longer be the heir. I am now the Countess of Cedarfell. The conversation was full of tears. I spent those six months traveling to a few of the different kingdoms on the continent, trying the different cuisines and seeing the different clothing styles of each kingdom. It was a marvelous experience. I loved the winter dresses of Zima, the summer dresses of Kallos, and the food in Luminaria is like a divine experience. It's the paperwork side of diplomacy I despise—and there is so much paperwork. I didn't realize how much boring busy work was involved in being an ambassador. I thought it would be more about traveling and trying to keep our allies happy with us. Nope. My hand clenches in memory of the last report I had to submit.

When we are both home, Roderick and I have been courting, which has been lovely for the most part. Roderick has been wonderful. The letters he has written when we are not in the same place are some of my most cherished possessions. But I think dancing under the full moon in Kallos by the ocean is undoubtedly the best memory I have of the past six months.

I hear someone walking behind me and turn around to see Gardenia. She has embraced the role of heir and future queen brilliantly. Naturally, there were skeptics. However, the past six months have shown them all how dedicated to our kingdom and how strong my sister really is. I am so proud of her.

"Itching to get back on the road already?" she asks me as she joins me in the Square Garden.

"No," I answer her honestly. "I mean, I am eager they've finished their renovations on Cedarfell Hall. I hope everything has gone according to plan with it."

"All reports have said as much," Gardenia says. Her nervousness is apparent, and in just a few moments, she will officially become the recognized heir of Verdant. Today, they will crown my sister as the heir of Verdant, and there will be a ball to celebrate, which she finds quite distressing. She did not get what she had asked for—a small ceremony and only a family dinner—but that doesn't surprise me. My sister hates being the center of attention. Nia would rather spend money helping our people than have a big party for herself. However, she will have to get used to it as the heir and eventually the queen.

But I know it isn't just being frugal with the kingdom's finances. Gardenia doesn't see herself the way the rest of us do. She is beautiful. She may not have the willowy frame a few of our sisters do, but that doesn't mean she isn't as beautiful as the rest of us. And her intelligence and goodness enhance her natural beauty.

"I know they have, but..." I hesitate to admit another truth.

"But?" she asks me with a raised eyebrow.

"But I want to go to Cedarfell with someone, not by myself," I answer her quietly. She arches an eyebrow at me with an understanding smile.

"Do you regret signing over your rights as the heir?" she asks me softly.

"Not for a moment."

We turn to head back towards the castle. I reach for her hand and give it a gentle squeeze. " It is you who will follow after Father, and it brings me joy, particularly because I am confident in your abilities to be a powerful queen. You know from our discussions in the council meetings, I have seen something in our neighboring kingdoms that, while not concerning yet, could become so, and you will face those challenges fabulously."

Along with my smile, I mention that I have no desire to be an ambassador.

From the owlish look she's giving me, I have shocked her, which brings me a little joy as her big sister.

"I love traveling and meeting people. However..." I roll my eyes skyward at the last word and shake my head, "I detest paperwork." I may have made the words more dramatic than necessary, but I can see they have the desired effect. She loses some of the tenseness in her shoulders and around her eyes.

"I am glad you're starting to be more of the you, you used to be," she says with a smile, and I know what she means. My former duties as the heir took over my life, and I wasn't myself. I aspired to be what my father wanted me to be, and those choices made me miserable. Becoming someone I didn't want to be was a challenging task for me. I have accepted that I am a daydreamer, but I don't allow it to take over the way it used to when I was miserable.

"Me too," I answer her. "You're going to be successful, and as long as you stay you, then we have nothing to worry about."

"Thank you, Hazel," she says softly as we enter the castle.

"You're welcome. However, we should probably return you to your room so you can get ready for the festivities."

The ceremony was flawless, and the celebratory ball for Gardenia is going brilliantly. The food is delicious, the music is lively, and the attendees all appear to be enjoying themselves. Everyone seems to be truly happy for my sister. There have been a few pitying looks thrown my way, but I don't mind. The people that give me those sad looks don't know how happy I am and how happy I am for my sister.

"You look beautiful," Roderick whispers in my ear. He found my hiding spot near a curtain by the patio doors of the ballroom and came up behind me. I turn around to look at him and can't help but sigh at how handsome he is. He is always handsome, but tonight, he's in his evening wear, which is a black suit with gold thread buttons and golden embellishments that make the coffee brown of his eyes pop, showing the gold flecks in them.

"You look very dashing," I say to him with a shy smile. "Have you been enjoying yourself this evening?"

"I have, and thank you," he says with a devilish grin. "But the evening would be better if you would take a walk through the gardens with me." He holds his hand out to me, and I delicately place mine in his. He moves it to his arm and escorts me around the dance floor and out the doors that lead to the circular garden. We wander the curving path of the garden and appreciate the round designs in silent wonder.

I want to be the one that tells him I'm no longer going to be an ambassador, but I'm not sure how he will take it. Hopefully, he doesn't perceive it as a slight on his chosen profession.

"I've already discussed it with my father," I begin, and I feel a blush come across my face that the setting sun is amplifying. "I will not be an ambassador," I tell him softly. "Instead, I will only be the Countess of Cedarfell Hall. I even asked Father to design a garden for my new home."

"I see," he says, and I look up and see a small frown on his face. He scrunches his brows and looks confused.

"I still want to go on adventures though," I say. "I'm just not a fan of paperwork," I tell him, and I can feel my blush deepen. This is awkward because this is how he has made a name for himself.

"How about you? How have your assignments been going?" I ask him, trying to salvage the moment.

"They have been going well. And they have assigned me a more permanent role."

"Really? That is so exciting. Do you know where?" I am trying to sound eager for him and be happy for him, but a small part of me is afraid he is going to say a distant kingdom, meaning I will hardly see him.

"It is an assignment," he says, brow furrowing, and he rubs his chin with his hand. Perhaps he doesn't want to tell me where. Have I messed up my chance with him because I don't aspire to be an ambassador myself?

He smiles at me and says, "Stop fretting, Hazel. Everything is going to be just fine." I give him a small smile in return, and we continue down the garden path.

"Before I tell you the location of my assignment, I want to make sure of something," he says.

"That sounds ominous. What do you want to know?" I cautiously ask him.

"Perhaps we should find a place to sit and talk," he says nervously. We decide to sit on the brim of the water fountain in the center of the circular garden. I am grateful the brim is wide enough that when I sit down on it, my gown does not get soaked instantly.

"What is it you want to talk about, Roderick?" My mind and heart are in a competition for which can go faster. He sits down next to me and angles himself so we can look at each other.

"You know I care for you," he says.

"Yes, and I you." My hands are sweating from nerves.

"But I want things to change," he says quietly, almost evasively, as if he is nervous.

"Change how?" I ask him. The confusion in my voice must also show on my face because he gives me a warm smile, like what someone gives you when they have news to share.

"We both have dreams of what the future might hold, and I'm wondering if our visions are the same," he says.

I blink at him, trying to keep the tears at bay. So I did mess this up. This is the end of our courtship. It hurts. I'm sure that eventually, I will be fine, but right now, I just want to disappear to my room and sob for the rest of the night.

"I see," I say, my voice going wobbly.

"You do?" he asks, and the smile leaves his face as he watches a tear run down my cheek. A look of deep sadness enters his eyes, causing them to look more like tree bark than coffee.

"You want to end our courtship?" I hiccup at the end because I am sobbing.

"What?" he exclaims as he jumps up from the brim of the fountain. "No, that is not what I want. Is it... Is it what you want?"

"No, but that's how it seems like this conversation is going."

"Ugh." He runs a hand roughly through his hair. "This is all going poorly. I am trying to ask you to marry me, Hazel."

"Oh!" I am so shocked that my body tries to process his words along with my mind, sending me from sitting to almost standing. But my feet get tangled in the hem of my gown. My arms are circling to keep my balance, but to no avail. I continue to swing backward and land in the fountain.

The frigid water splashes around me. I am entirely submerged. *Thank you to my short stature.* As I break the surface, I hear Roderick calling my name as he joins me in the fountain.

"Hazel, are you alright?" he asks me frantically.

I wipe the water from my eyes, and when I see him looking so concerned, his own shoes and pants soaked, I laugh. He offers me a hand, and I accept it, then pull him further into the water. It is only fair. He startled me into falling into the fountain after all.

When he wipes the water from his face and gives me a grin, I lean towards him and say, "Yes." I grab his shirt to pull him to me and eyes meet as I move my face towards his. The look in his eyes sends a warm feeling from my heart through my body to my fingers and toes. I press my lips against his.

It might not be the most romantic proposal, but it suits me. We break apart, and I am ecstatic—and cold. It is the middle of autumn, so the days are comfortable but not warm enough for swimming.

"Should we get out of the fountain?" he asks me with a laugh.

"I think that would be best," my father says darkly.

We both jump, but I fall back into the water, thanks to the extra added weight of my gown.

"Hazel," Father begins. He covers the short distance from the turn in the circular garden to the center where the fountain is in admirable time. He looks at me and my soaked state and laughs a full, body-shaking guffaw. I love my father, but his laugh is not what one would consider typical. Not all of his daughters inherited his awkward chuckle, but I certainly did. From what I can tell, so have Peony, Jasmine, and Iris. Our laugh is more of the awkward chuckle variety. It is a peculiar sound that is a mix of chuckling and wheezing.

Roderick kindly helps me from the fountain when the skirt of my dress hits the stones with a splat. Father almost cries from laughing harder. When Father regains control of himself, he asks, "Have you two settled things? I assume you approve of his placement as ambassador."

"We hadn't got to that part yet," Roderick answers him sheepishly.

"But I accepted his proposal."

"Well, I think she'll like the location of your assignment very well," Father says vaguely.

"I agree, Your Majesty," Roderick replies with a smile.

With shivering and chattering teeth, I ask, "What location?"

"I am glad she accepted your suit," Father says. "It wouldn't be nearly as interesting if she hadn't caused a scene, though."

"Yes, I apologize. I made a mess of things," Roderick says solemnly.

"I'm sure you weren't alone in the scene I walked in upon."

"No, he wasn't. I'm just as guilty," I stutter out between teeth chattering and ask again, "Which kingdom?"

"If I am being honest with you, sir, it is one of reasons I love her. I know life will not be dull with her in it."

"That is true," Father chuckles, "but perhaps we should move this conversation indoors. You two refresh yourselves and meet us back in the ballroom."

"This is—thank you," I stutter, "but what kingdom?"

"Norland," Roderick answers.

Norland. My estate is close to the border of Norland. I look at Roderick, then my father, and have to fight back tears of joy. He will be close to me even when he's away at work.

Once I am dried off and in a not-so-soaked dress, I make my way back down to the ball, celebrating my sister, who is trying to make an escape as I'm entering.

"Are you trying to leave already?" I ask her.

She mumbles, "I just need a brief break."

"What was said?"

"Do not trouble yourself with it, sister. You have a wonderful fiancé waiting for you in the ballroom," Nia answers me.

"That may be, but I want to know what someone said that led you to leave your own ball."

She sighs, then says, "I overheard some councilors telling father I will need a powerful husband to keep the throne."

"They said what?"

"I can handle this, I promise. Please do not worry about it. I would, however," she gives me a cheeky grin, "like to see you dance with my future brother-in-law."

"I won't promise to not worry about you, but I can promise to dance with Roderick tonight."

We enter the ballroom with smiles and let the naysayers say what they want. This is a night for celebrating. I look around the room and see Roderick has also changed and is speaking with Father and Sabrina. The thought occurs to me: why was Father in the garden? I ask Gardenia, and she laughs before answering.

"We all knew Roderick was planning to propose tonight. Father aspired to be the first to congratulate you, but I'm guessing from the change of wardrobe being necessary, Father got more than he wanted."

I blush at her comment, and we walk to where Father, Sabrina, and Roderick are all talking. I whisper to her, "Nothing untoward happened."

"Congratulations, Hazel," Sabrina says with a big smile and gives me a hug.

"Thank you," I say as I return her hug. I look at my father when Sabrina and I step apart. "I am sorry for the spectacle you arrived at, Father."

He smiles and says, "All is well, and congratulations to you, Hazel and Roderick. I think what *they*," he nods towards the guests at the ball, "need is for you two to dance."

"I would hate to disappoint *them*," Roderick says.

"Yes, it would be horrible of us." I cannot stop my grin. Roderick smiles, bows to me, and holds out a hand. After he rises back up, I curtsy and place my hand in his, smiling at him with a grin that stretches from cheek to cheek. Just as we reach the dance floor, the band begins a waltz. We step together and spin; it is honestly a magical moment.

As we are completing another turn, Roderick whispers to me, "We could shock them all, you know."

"How?" I ask him.

"I could kiss you."

"I would let you," I whisper after a moment.

"Oh, really?" he asks with a mischievous grin.

"Hmm," I answer.

Roderick stops us in the middle of the dance and brings me closer to him, closer than society would prefer. He raises his hand to tip my chin up. He leans forward, and I close my eyes as his lips meet mine. The startled gasp of those at the ball makes me snort. It is so definitely worth the gossip because I am getting what I wished for: an adventure with my true love.

The end.

Thank You

First, to God: thank you for everything—the inspiration for my stories, the words to fill them, and the readers to enjoy them.

Thank you, Anabel, Ashley, and Robyn! Your feedback has been invaluable, and I truly appreciate each of you.

Meghan Kleinschmidt, your guidance and editing skills deserve praise—you are amazing. Thank you!

To my daughter, thank you for helping choose the perfect fairy tale for Hazel's story.

To my parents, thank you for your love, support, and encouragement.

To the wonderful cover artist team at GET COVERS, thank you!

And again, to God: I thank you daily for your love and mercy.

About the Author

Amanda Thompson is a small-town girl with the love of books, just like a certain princess in a certain movie that came out over thirty years ago. But unlike that lucky girl, Amanda doesn't have a castle with talking clocks or candelabras. But with her fear of technology taking over the world, thanks to a different movie, Amanda is glad she doesn't have the talking appliances. She does, however, have a teenage daughter that she loves deeply and a cat named Spock. If Amanda is not working at her day job, writing her latest idea, reading someone else's wonderful work, you can find her spending time with her family. Or trying to win the war against the villain known as laundry. Amanda is a lover of clean, sweet fairy tales, and fantasy and that is what she promises to do her best at writing.

AMANDA THOMPSON

A FRIGID HOPE

A SNOW QUEEN RETELLING

HOPE EVER AFTER

A Frigid Hope

A Snow Queen
Retelling

Can one princess find hope before her best friend's heart is turned to ice?

Every year a man is chosen to make the journey up the forbidden mountain to appease the Frozen Queen, only to return with a frozen heart. When Crown Princess Bianca learns her best friend is this year's chosen, she is devastated. And she's willing to do anything to save Percival from that fate.

Percival's heartbroken when he finds the mark selecting him to be this year's chosen. He's Bianca's personal guard – and he has been in love with her for years. But with the selection mark comes a warning: to disobey means death, not just for him but for everyone in the kingdom.

Can Bianca save her people from the endless winter and prevent Percival from losing his heart? Or will all be lost to the frigid reign of the Frozen Queen?

AMANDA THOMPSON

The
Caring
and the
Cursed

THE INTERTWINED TALES

THE CARING AND THE CURSED

A PUSS IN BOOTS AND SNOW WHITE & ROSE RED RETELLING

A cursed prince. A miller's daughter who is willing to do anything to save her family. Are they the only hope to save their kingdom?

When Crown Prince Alexander is cursed into the form of a cat, he fears all is lost. Little does he know that when he stumbles upon two sisters he has found his sweetest and bravest companions.

Eirwen loves her family deeply and is willing to enter into a loveless and miserable marriage for their sake. Neither she nor her younger sister, Rowan, will inherit the mill so this is how she can do her part.

When a talking cat scares them both, Eirwen is afraid that evil has come to destroy her family. But is he really an evil cat, or is it possible there's more to meet the eye with this new furry friend? And is he someone she could have a

future with and not be miserable?

Can these two sisters aid the talking cat in facing off against the evil that is plaguing their country, or are they all doomed for more curses?

DANCES
AND
DANGER

A TWELVE DANCING
PRINCESSES RETELLING

AMANDA THOMPSON

Dances and Danger
A Twelve Dancing Princesses Retelling

A tournament, a threat, and a terrifying dance.

Princess Gardenia loves her life, her family, and her kingdom. Being heir to the throne is a challenge she enjoys. Her father throwing a tourney to find her a husband, while not a joy, is something she can handle. If only the eyes she has dreamed of for months were easier to forget. However, Nia doesn't get to daydream because she must focus on saving her sisters and herself from being forced to dance until exhaustion every night. As Nia watches her sisters fade, she wonders if she is truly fit to be the future

queen—and if she'll survive long enough to be crowned. Prince Dario of Cortes is eager to prove himself as capable as his older brother. Craving adventure, he hopes the tournament will allow him to do just that—and possibly find love. If the feelings he has for a certain beautiful princess are anything to go by, he has possibly found his soulmate. But befriending the princesses puts the twelve young ladies in even more peril, and soon the princesses

are fighting new dangers against threats seen and unseen.
Can the curse be broken before it's too late? Or will the princesses be forced to dance until they each fade from existence?

Also By

Hope Ever After Series

A Frigid Hope: A Snow Queen Retelling

(Also a prequel to the Fairy Tales of Ambrose)

The Intertwined Tales

The Caring and the Cursed: A Puss in Boots and Snow White & Rose Red Retelling

(Also a prequel to the Fairy Tales of Ambrose)

The Fairy Tales of Ambrose

Amphibians and Admiration: A Frog Prince Retelling (Prequel)

Dances and Danger: A Twelve Dancing Princesses Retelling (Book One of the Fairy Tales of Ambrose)

Promises and Poison: A Gender Flipped Snow White Retelling (Book Two of the Fairy Tales of Ambrose)

www.ingramcontent.com/pod-product-compliance
Lightning Source LLC
Chambersburg PA
CBHW022038170626
46808CB00003B/1267